GROOVY JOE

If You're GROOVY and You Know It, Hug a Friend!

STORY AND PERFORMANCE BY **Eric Litwin**   illustrated by **Tom Lichtenheld**

Orchard Books

An Imprint of Scholastic Inc.

New York

If you're groovy and you know it, greet the day!

If you're groovy
and you know it,
the things you do
will show it!

If you're groovy
and you know it,
greet the day!

If you're groovy
    and you know it,
go explore!

If you're groovy
   and you know it,
go explore!

If you're groovy
  and you know it,
the things you do
  will show it!

If you're groovy
  and you know it,
  go explore!

If you're groovy and you know it, laugh and play!

If you're groovy
and you know it,
laugh and play!

If you're groovy
and you know it,
the things you do
will show it!

If you're groovy
and you know it,
laugh and play!

If you're groovy
and you know it,
plant a seed!

If you're groovy and you know it, plant a seed!

If you're groovy
   and you know it,
the things you do
   will show it!

If you're groovy
and you know it,
plant a seed.

If you're groovy
   and you know it,
read a book!

If you're groovy
   and you know it,
read a book!

If you're groovy
and you know it,
the things you do
will show it!

If you're groovy
and you know it,
read a book!

We're all ears!

If you're groovy
    and you know it,
sing your song!

If you're groovy
    and you know it,
sing your song!

If you're groovy
and you know it,
the things you do
will show it!

If you're groovy
and you know it,
sing your song!

If you're groovy
and you know it,
hug a friend!

If you're groovy
and you know it,
hug a friend!

If you're groovy
and you know it,
the things you do
will show it!

If you're groovy
and you know it,
hug a friend!

If You're Groovy and You Know It

Sing to the tune of "If You're Happy and You Know It"

If you're groovy and you know it, greet the day. (Hello, day!)
   If you're groovy and you know it, greet the day. (Hello, day!)
If you're groovy and you know it, the things you do will show it.
   If you're groovy and you know it, greet the day. (Hello, day!)

If you're groovy and you know it, go explore. (Out the door!)
   If you're groovy and you know it, go explore. (Out the door!)
If you're groovy and you know it, the things you do will show it.
   If you're groovy and you know it, go explore. (Out the door!)

If you're groovy and you know it, laugh and play. (Hip hip hooray!)
   If you're groovy and you know it, laugh and play. (Hip hip hooray!)
If you're groovy and you know it, the things you do will show it.
   If you're groovy and you know it, laugh and play. (Hip hip hooray!)

If you're groovy and you know it, plant a seed. (Yes indeed!)
   If you're groovy and you know it, plant a seed. (Yes indeed!)
If you're groovy and you know it, the things you do will show it.
   If you're groovy and you know it, plant a seed. (Yes indeed!)

If you're groovy and you know it, read a book. (Take a look!)
   If you're groovy and you know it, read a book. (Take a look!)
If you're groovy and you know it, the things you do will show it.
   If you're groovy and you know it, read a book. (Take a look!)

If you're groovy and you know it, sing your song. (Let's sing along!)
   If you're groovy and you know it, sing your song. (Let's sing along!)
If you're groovy and you know it, the things you do will show it.
   If you're groovy and you know it, sing your song. (Let's sing along!)

If you're groovy and you know it, hug a friend. (Once again!)
   If you're groovy and you know it, hug a friend. (Once again!)
If you're groovy and you know it, the things you do will show it.
   If you're groovy and you know it, hug a friend. (Once again!)

My Brilliant, Resilient Mind

How to Ditch Negative Thinking
to Handle Hard Things Better

Christina Furnival

ILLUSTRATED BY Katie Dwyer

My Brilliant, Resilient Mind
Copyright © 2023 by Christina Furnival

Published by:
PESI Publishing, Inc.
3839 White Ave
Eau Claire, WI 54703

Illustrations and Cover: Katie Dwyer
Layout: Katie Dwyer, Amy Rubenzer

ISBN 9781683736684 (print)
ISBN 9781683736691 (ePUB)
ISBN 9781683736707 (ePDF)
ISBN 9781683736714 (KPF)

PESI Publishing
pesipublishing.com

Dedication

To my littles, that you may forever harness
the power of your thoughts to work through
challenges and create the lives you want.

There once were two twins,
quite like you and like me.
They were loved, they were funny—
as smart as could be.

They had a nice family,
a handful of mates.
He liked art, she loved soccer.
They both had good traits.

Then life threw some curveballs,
which life tends to do.
It was hard and confusing.
They felt kind of blue.

She became somewhat gloomy
and down in the dumps.

His mood was directed
by life's lumps and bumps.

In this doom-and-gloom state,
they just couldn't bounce back.
They were stuck on a negative, unhappy track.

But these twins were determined to muster their strength,
to reset their minds on a whole new wavelength.

You see, what they realized, when they thought of their thoughts
(which is really a thing we should do quite a lot),
was their style of thinking wasn't helping them out.
Their negative thoughts filled them both with self-doubt.

 Mindset: What you believe about yourself and your experiences

Their mindset and what they thought under the lid
shaped both how they felt and whatever they did.
Their mindset impacted their moods and their choices,
so they reframed and shifted their inner-most voices.

Let's look at that game
when the other team won...
She believed it was *her* fault—
self-talk had begun.
Her thoughts said, "I'm no good!
We lost 'cause of me!"
But that wasn't true—
they had worked as a team.

Unhelpful Thinking Style: Personalization or **I Blame Myself**
Solution: Remind yourself that there are lots of other reasons why things happen.

She reflected again,
in a self-loving fashion,
and reframed her thoughts,
showing herself compassion.
"I made some mistakes,
but I won't get all stressed.
We all played with heart and
we all tried our best."

With a shift in her thinking from stinking to sweet,
she worked through the feelings brought on by defeat.
She gained some perspective—a new point of view
with thoughts that were helpful and even more true.

Or how 'bout the time (there are probably lots)
that his littlest sis had some not-so-nice plots.

"She *always* is like this!
She *never* is nice."

This style of thinking is called black-and-white.

 Unhelpful Thinking Style: Black-and-White or **All-or-Nothing Thinking**
Solution: Remind yourself that things are very rarely "always" or "never."

He thought in extremes, which just made him feel worse, but he realized these thoughts were a negative curse. Reshaping his thoughts with more big-picture thinking helped grow his perspective and kept it from shrinking.

"I don't like that she did that, and while it's not okay...
she's younger, she's learning, she's not often this way."
With his mindset evolving, he's starting to see
that it's not all-or-nothing, but more in-between.

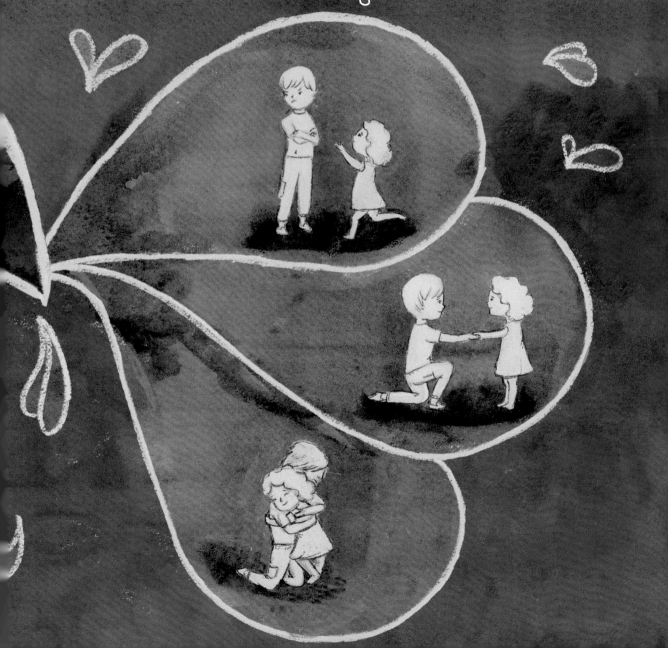

Or the move this last year to a new and strange place...
she couldn't believe her "despicable" fate.
She focused on bad, like good didn't exist.
And anything happy was ignored or dismissed.

"This neighborhood's weird, and this house is so bare.
I miss my old friends, oh, it feels so unfair."
She noticed her thoughts were all shadowed and dark,
so she started rethinking to regain her spark.

"I miss our old home.
And this new one is fine.
I miss my old friends.
And I'll make some in time."
It's okay to feel sad and
to sit in that feeling...
and to notice the good—
it will speed up the healing.

Or the project for school hanging over his head...
to him it looked wrong, and it filled with him dread.

His thoughts were critiques:
"I *must* be the best."
"I *should* do it better
than all of the rest."

Unhelpful Thinking Style: "Shoulds & Musts"
a.k.a **Perfection or Bust**

Solution: Remind yourself that "perfect" doesn't exis
and that effort matters more than outcome.

He felt like a failure, was full of disgust.
He thought, "I'll give up—it's perfection or bust."

But he disliked the pressure from thoughts so judgmental,
so he changed them to ones that were kind, fair, and gentle.

"I made some mistakes,
but I *did* do my best.
I hope that my teacher
will still be impressed."

He's learning his effort
is what makes him great,
that perfect's not real,
and to grow from mistakes.

The life of the twins has improved quite a lot.
Amazing—it all had to do with their thoughts!

Their lives have bounced back
from (in *their* minds) "disaster."
With a new way of thinking,
they're mind and thought masters.

When things feel unfair and it all seems so tough,
just know that you and your mind are enough.

With a mindset that's growing, that's wise and reflective,
you can see from more angles and gain some perspective.

No matter what happens, you can think of your thoughts and recognize whether they're helpful or *not*.

You can reframe your thoughts—they really are shapeable—
and then you will realize: You *really* are capable!

Note to Parents and Professionals

This story in the *Capable Kiddos* series involves the topics of cognitive distortions (which are also known as *stinking thinking*) and cognitive restructuring (which involves reframing unhelpful thoughts to healthier, more helpful ones).

If you are a parent or caregiver, or you work with children, you've seen children get in their own way and make their struggles worse. Maybe your child gives up when they can't do things perfectly, or they're afraid to try new things due to fear of failure. Maybe your child lives in negativity land—often discounting the positives in their life—or maybe they feel like life is always unfair.

My Brilliant, Resilient Mind is the antidote to these poisonous styles of thinking, as it empowers children to cope with life's stressors by developing a more compassionate and balanced way of thinking—equipping them to handle whatever challenges life throws their way.

Conversation Starters and Discussion Questions

- **What is a brilliant, resilient mind?**

  The word *brilliant* means clever and marvelous, and *resilient* means that you are able to bounce back from challenges. Your brilliant, resilient mind is both smart and capable, and it is constantly evolving and improving as you learn and grow!

- **What is a mindset?**

  A mindset is how you think about things, including what you believe about yourself, others, and the world. Your mindset has the ability to help you feel positive, even when things are tough, as well as the ability to make you feel worse. We now know that mindsets are *not* so "set"—meaning you can mold your mindset to be more helpful to you by paying attention to your thoughts.

- **What do my thoughts have to do with the ups and downs of life?**

  We are all unique, and we all have our own thoughts and feelings about what happens in our lives. As an example, two people can experience the exact same event but have very different thoughts about what happened. One person may think about the event in a negative way, causing them to feel down, while the other person may think about it in a more helpful and balanced way, which enhances their resilience and empowers them to push onward.

- **What are cognitive distortions?**

  A cognitive distortion is a clinical term that describes distorted, unhelpful, or misleading ways of thinking. The thing about thoughts is that they are not always true! Your thoughts are based on your own beliefs and opinions, but not always on actual fact. Distorted thoughts inaccurately shape how you perceive your life, which negatively impacts the choices you make, often making the situation even worse.

  Everyone experiences cognitive distortions on occasion, but when they become your go-to thinking approach, the hard parts of life feel even harder, and you can feel stuck. To understand more about the types of cognitive distortions, check out the "Rethinking Stinking Thinking" section at the end of this book. This will help you see if you lean toward one style of unhelpful thinking and then can help you reframe them.

- **Why should I practice thinking about thinking?**

  In your busy life, you probably don't stop to think about your thoughts too often, but you should, since you can't believe everything you think! Thinking about your thoughts may feel challenging at first, but like other skills, the more you do it, the better you get. When you think about thinking, you're better able to notice the types of thoughts you are having, which is the first step toward recognizing if you are using cognitive distortions.

- **How do I go about reframing unhelpful thoughts?**

1. Think about your thoughts and determine if they are helping you or making things harder.

2. If your thoughts are making things harder, identify which type of cognitive distortion or unhelpful thinking style you are using.

3. Notice how these thoughts are making you feel on a scale of 1 to 10 (where 1 = "not bothered at all" and 10 = "extremely upset").

4. Get curious about your thoughts. Are these thoughts true? If a friend had these same thoughts about the situation, what would you say to them? What evidence proves *and* disproves the unhelpful thoughts?

5. Name alternate thoughts you could have about the situation that *are* true and more helpful. Notice how these thoughts make you feel using the same rating scale from 1 to 10. You'll likely see that your alternative thoughts don't make you feel so bad, and from there, you can make better, safer, and more rewarding choices.

Rethinking Stinking Thinking

Here are the top 10 cognitive distortions that affect kids like you, along with suggestions for how to reframe them. Everyone has these unhelpful thoughts from time to time, but it up to you to notice when they pop up and to practice reframing them into more helpful ways of thinking. So let's learn how!

1. "I Blame Myself" (Personalization)

This thinking style involves taking things personally or blaming yourself for something that is largely out of your control.

How to reframe: Remind yourself that there are lots of other reasons why things happen. In the best way, the world does not revolve around you, meaning that it is very rare that something is entirely your fault!

2. "All-or-Nothing Thinking" (Black-and-White Thinking)

With all-or-nothing thinking, you view things in extremes: Things are always good or bad, right or wrong. This is also called black-and-white thinking because you think in terms of opposites.

How to reframe: Remind yourself that rarely are things in life black and white, always or never. There is much more gray in-between.

3. "Negativity Glasses" (Mental Filter)

When you put on dark glasses, it makes the whole world look darker, doesn't it? The problem is, when you make it a habit to focus on what's *not* going well, negativity grows and grows until it's all you can see.

How to reframe: When you catch yourself looking for the bad ("That's not fair!"), make an effort to notice the good instead. I promise it's out there.

4. "Perfection or Bust" (Shoulds and Musts)

This style of thinking involves holding yourself (or others) to unrealistic standards, which sets you up to feel like a failure (or to blame others).

How to reframe: Remember that effort matters more than outcome. Look at mistakes as learning opportunities to help you grow your skills and abilities.

5. "False Future" (Jumping to Conclusions)

When you jump to conclusions, you make guesses about what someone else might be thinking, or you make predictions about what might happen in the future. The problem with this thinking style is that people sometimes (often!) assume incorrectly.

How to reframe: Remind yourself that there is no way you can know *for sure* what is going on in someone else's head, unless you ask them. It's also impossible to predict the future—you can only hope for the best and do your part to make the best outcome a reality.

6. "Slime Spread" (Overgeneralizing)

This thinking style involves taking one negative experience—which happened at one moment in time, under specific circumstances—and applying it to other (often unrelated) events. It's like slime, which has a way of spreading out and covering a bigger area.

How to reframe: Remind yourself that just because something bad happened once doesn't mean that it will keep happening over and over again.

7. "Emotion-Controlled Brain" (Emotional Reasoning)

When you have an emotion-controlled brain, you treat your feelings as facts. For example, if you *feel* scared about meeting a new friend, you assume that you really *are* in danger.

How to reframe: The next time you find yourself making conclusions based on your emotions (instead of looking at the facts), try telling yourself, "Just because I feel this way, it doesn't make it true." You don't need to mistake your feelings for facts.

8. "Name Calling" (Labeling)

This distortion involves calling yourself mean names based on your behavior in a single situation. For example, you might do poorly on a test and say, "I am so dumb" or "I am a failure."

How to reframe: Describe the facts of what happened, without judgments or opinions. ("I didn't do well on the test.")

9. "Yeah, Whatever" (Disqualifying the Positive)

When you shut down the positives with statements like "Yeah, whatever, that doesn't count," you prevent yourself from celebrating your triumphs and noticing the good.

How to reframe: Practice noticing and accepting the good things that you have done or contributed to, even if it feels uncomfortable at first.

10. "Blowing Things Up" (Catastrophizing)

With this thinking style, you blow things out of proportion and assume that the worst possible outcome is likely to occur.

How to reframe: Ask yourself: What is the worst that could *really* happen? Then remind yourself of all the strengths you have to handle whatever comes your way.

About the Author

Christina Furnival, MS, LPCC, is a mom to three young children, a licensed mental health therapist, and an author of several children's books and therapy tools. Her award-winning and best-selling social-emotional children's book series, *Capable Kiddos*, is inspired by the families she helps, as well as her own children. Fusing her professional background and experience with her personal journey through motherhood, she is able to provide a therapist's perspective with evidence-backed tools for the everyday challenges that parents and their children face. When not occupied by work and passion projects, Christina can be found with her husband and children having fun at the beach, baking in the kitchen, tackling DIY renovations, and singing and dancing wildly in their family room.

About the Illustrator

Katie Dwyer is a children's book illustrator living in the magical woods of Asheville, North Carolina, with her husband and three wildlings. She loves illustrating stories that teach valuable lessons while adding a twist of whimsical charm. When she's not drawing or painting in her studio, she can be found drinking iced matcha lattes with her nose in a book or watching a good movie. Visit her at katiedwyerillustrations.com or on Instagram @katiedwyer.illustrations.

Also in the *Capable Kiddos Series*